BENEATH the BLUSHING SKY

A COMING-OF-AGE STORY

GARY McILROY

Beneath the Blushing Sky

Copyright ©2025
Publisher: Oscar Publications

ISBN paperback: 979-8-9923742-0-9
ISBN e-book: 979-8-9923742-1-6

This novel is entirely a work of fiction. The names, characters and incidents portrayed in it are the work of the author's imagination. Any resemblance to actual persons, living or dead, events or localities is entirely coincidental.

To Monica,
another kind

The thing about basketball is that it's not about basketball.

Bill Simmons

Acknowledgments

I owe an immense debt of gratitude to Monica Dewey, whose feedback and editorial assistance were invaluable, and to Michael McColl, whose mastery of prose and poetry has been my guiding light for many years. I am also indebted to all of my former teammates and coaches, especially my sixth-grade teacher and coach, James Wisdom, who first instilled in me a love for the game.

Beneath the Blushing Sky

Circa 1965

PART I

Jim Miller was smiling. He had plopped himself down on a worn leather seat of a school bus. His best friend Lee sat just across the aisle. The bus was taking the Wilford Creek Junior High's ninth-grade basketball team across town to play a game against its fiercest rival. "Lee . . . Lee," he whispered, not wanting Coach to hear, "want to play pool tomorrow?" Lee nodded. It was a miracle that Jim was making any plans, but his father had not yet discovered the dent in the family car, the one Jim had put there the previous weekend when he had taken the car out without permission. He had waited for his father to fall asleep, rolled the car down the driveway, and then started it on the street, a full year before he could even obtain a driver's permit.

Jim hadn't always been Lee's best friend. In seventh grade, when it looked like they would be battling for the same position on the basketball team, they were rivals. "You're better than he is," declared one of Lee's friends, but Lee wasn't so sure. Although he was only thirteen, Jim possessed the rugged, broad-shouldered physique of a mature athlete.

As the bus pulled away from school, Lee studied the sky. All day it had been overcast and gray, as if nature had rented a billboard to say "Unwelcome." But inside the bus it was lively. Everyone was excited about the game and the weekend ahead, everyone but Coach, who sat in the front row craning his neck to see out the windshield. He could trust no one, not even this veteran bus driver, to get them to the game on time. Although the team had won their first three games, Coach was not satisfied. They still had to face their toughest opponents.

Coach had instructed the players to be quiet, to visualize how they would perform in today's game, but they were restless, rambunctious. In the back row, Phil Novak slipped a jockstrap over Tom Solomon's head and the two had begun to tussle. Closer to the front, Brad Simmons chucked a Lifesaver at Chris Ward, which hit the metal seat frame and burst into tiny flakes of orange.

Coach could take it no longer. He strode halfway down the aisle, raised his clipboard, and brought it smartly down on Brad Simmons' head. "This is not the way we prepare for an important game!" he shouted, his thick neck muscles straining against his shirt collar, his veins trembling and purplish.

The brakes of the bus screeched in indignant sympathy. They had stopped at a traffic light in the middle of town. No one moved. Or breathed. Seconds ticked away. Minutes vanished. The moment needed closure, but the light would not change. Desperate for movement or progression, Lee's mind was off and running: Jefferson wrote the Declaration, Washington crossed the Delaware, Glen orbited the earth, Opie fell in love, but still the light would not change.

And just when it seemed certain that the fun was over—the game, the bus trip home, and even the week-end ahead—a flood of sunlight broke through the clouds illuminating the north side of the street. The dingy, red-brick buildings, or so they appeared just seconds before, now glowed with warmth and intimacy. Crystal deposits in the sidewalks sparkled like fresh-cut diamonds, a flag unfurled above a storefront, and second story windows shone like newborn suns. Then, as if on cue, a sparrow alighted on a street lamp, carrying in its beak the tiniest of twigs. This delicate, diminutive creature—so richly brown on top, so lightly feathered underneath, so wary, clear-eyed, and keen—was proof of some momentous transformation of the world. An entirely benign force was toying with perfection.

Inside the bus it was lighter, too. The tension of the previous moment had vanished. Coach's eyes had lost their menace and his pale blue shirt collar rested more softly on his neck. In fact, when he started to speak again, it was with such a softer tone that Lee at first thought he was going to apologize. He had never been more mistaken.

"Guys, let me tell you a secret. Nobody gives a rat's ass about this team. You're not little kids anymore, so you're not cute, and you're not old enough for the games to actually mean something. You're stuck here in between, and, unfortunately, I'm stuck here with you. So unless you keep your mouths shut and demonstrate that you are serious about playing on this team, I am going to make you wish that you'd never gotten on this bus today."

It was not surprising that Wilford Creek won the game or that Coach's angry outburst on the way there was already being made light of on the way back. But like most of his furious tirades, it would not soon be forgotten. Nor for Lee would the sudden and breathtaking way the light had fallen on that city block. If Coach had a secret, then Lee had one too, even if he could not put his into words.

hortly after finishing his TV dinner and throwing out the empty container and rinsing his glass in the sink and finally settling down at the kitchen table and opening his math book to page 83, exercise 14, Lee Rollins thought he heard someone knocking at the front door. Sure enough, when he opened it, he saw Carmen, Lisa, and Katie just standing there, all smiles, like maybe he should have been expecting them.

"Hi, Lee! Can we come in?"

Come in? What planet am I on? These girls show up out of nowhere and expect to come in?

"For what?" Lee shouted through the storm door. In his defense, it was the middle of the week, and such intrusions were rare, even on weekends.

"To talk," Lisa answered cheerfully.

So, sitting in his living room with Carmen, the most popular girl in ninth grade, and Lisa and Katie, cheerleaders he has had crushes on since God knows when, he felt like a tiny goldfish on display. His cereal bowl from two days before sat on the edge of the coffee table, his mother's frayed slippers peeked out shyly from under the couch, and piles of newspapers lay in floppy stacks all over the floor.

"You won't believe what happened to Katie today," Lisa blurted out, as if the girls had rushed over to Lee's house just to tell him this news. "She was playing kick-ball in gym class, and one of the balls got stuck on the top of the bleachers. It wasn't even her fault!"

Shrieking with laughter, she struggled to speak. "The teacher was gone, I mean in her office or something, so she tried to climb to the top to get it and her shorts split, and some of the boys on the other side saw her!" Katie covered her face in humiliation, and all three girls rocked back and forth in helpless convulsions.

Carmen was the first to recover. "Lee, how are you? I didn't see you in school today."

He could have hugged her for trying to keep the conversation going, but his morning had been so mixed up with his parents' quarreling that he had no way of getting to school on time. "I'm fine," he replied, ignoring the part about school. Then, after an awkward silence in which not one of the girls so much as brushed back a hair, Lee added something that would embarrass him even years later: "I grew an inch and a quarter last year, and my doctor thinks I'm going to be 5'10" someday."

Mercifully, the girls appear not to have heard him, or maybe they just didn't care. Instead, they huddled as if calling a play. It didn't take long, however, before Katie got up and approached his chair. "Lee, could I talk to you for a minute?"

This is it, he thought. This is what it's all about. He followed her into the kitchen, past his abandoned homework. His lips were dry, and his legs felt weak. Of course, he knew a lot about "making out" if certain self-proclaimed experts of his acquaintance could be trusted, but he was a little confused about how long it lasted and the protocol for stopping. What he hadn't anticipated was that his first time would be in his own kitchen amongst the Tupperware and dish towels.

Then the phone rang—sharply, urgently. Lee pivoted toward the wall and picked up the receiver. "Lee, honey, it's Mom. I had to work late, and now I have to see some-body. Are you all right? Good. Did you eat? Good. I'll be home in an hour."

CLICK.

Not one for long conversations, his mother. When she called from the hospital the night his grandmother died, she said only, "Lee, I have bad news. Grandma passed away. There was nothing they could do. After I sign some papers, I'll be home. Do you understand?"

CLICK.

The clicks, he imagined, were her goodbyes. An occasional double click was an especially fond goodbye. As a child, Lee would cry every time his mother left the house, and though he was far beyond such dependence now, he always felt better when she was home.

With no other options, he turned to face his pursuer.

Wasting no time, she grabbed his hands, looked him in the eyes, and addressed him as if they had been best friends their entire lives.

"Lee, you've got to do this for me! You just have to!"

He had no idea what she was talking about.

"You've got to take Carmen to the dance or at least meet her there."

Her eyes pleaded for him to agree. "Really, Lee. She wants you to take her. Please, please, please!"

This time the dance was cool. Way cool. It wasn't like the silly pretend dances of seventh grade or that stupid Halloween party in eighth. This time the cafeteria didn't look like the same old cafeteria except for paper decorations covering light switches and air vents. This time you could hardly tell it was a cafeteria. Murals of city nightscapes had been painted on room dividers, floor lamps had replaced the overhead lighting, and every table had a tablecloth, a candle, and a fistful of flowers.

Although Lee's mother had insisted on taking pictures, it wasn't so bad. Carmen's mother was their chauffeur, and she was one of the few parents who didn't ask too many questions. Lee hadn't thought of buying a corsage, but his mother had purchased one, which saved the day. Lee and Carmen arrived early and secured a good table. In a pastel pink velvet dress with long sleeves, Carmen was adorable, possessing an all-American sweetness that could have landed her on the cover of *Seventeen* magazine. By contrast, though neatly attired in a blue sports jacket and tailored gray pants, Lee looked decidedly younger than his date (as well as an inch shorter), though his good manners, cheerful disposition, and dimpled smile were ample compensation.

The excitement increased as more students arrived. The girls were happy to show off their dresses while the guys were relieved to have other guys to talk to. Lee was proud that he had agreed to come and was beginning to think he might enjoy himself. Unfortunately, that hope was short-lived. A rumor that had begun circulating on the other side of the room finally made its way to him. Jim Miller was in trouble. At first it wasn't clear what he had done (the stories were as varied as they were sensational) but a boy whose father worked for the county seemed to have the most authoritative account. In brief, Jim had been arrested for assisting in a robbery. He had allegedly diverted the attention of a store clerk while a group of older boys made off with several cartons of cigarettes and a case of liquor. Lee couldn't fathom it. Jim had no shortage of friends and always seemed to have money for whatever he needed. Sure, he was a risk-taker and could be easily bored, but his life at present didn't seem especially dull or uneventful. However, it occurred to Lee that since Jim was being recruited by some upperclassmen to play varsity football next year, this could have been some kind of initiation. Maybe Carmen could explain it. She and Jim had grown up in the same neighborhood, and they were close. But where was she? Earlier he had seen her darting from one group of girls to another. Now he couldn't find her anywhere.

She finally returned to their table when the music

started. She too had heard the rumors about Jim but was sure they were false. Or perhaps she was just shielding herself from an unpleasant reality. "Thanks for bringing me," she whispered in Lee's ear. "I'm sorry if I forced you." Lee protested vehemently. He hadn't been forced at all. Whether this was true was beside the point, but as the night unfolded he would have reason to doubt her sincerity. After listening to the music for a while and even dancing to two of the slower numbers, the couple made their way to a private corner. Everything seemed fine until Lee noticed that Carmen was keenly observing an animated discussion on the other side of the room. It was between Katie and a boy Lee did not recognize. Most likely, he was just some high school sophomore trying to impress a younger girl. It was only when they rejoined the others that things became confusing. The girls spoke only in whispers and kept retreating to the restroom for greater privacy. At one point, Katie returned to his table, chatting amicably (though point-lessly) until she was summoned back by the others. It was getting late. The fluorescent lights had been turned on and everyone was heading toward the exits. Finally, Katie strode over to Lee's table one last time to make the following pronouncement: "Lisa's mother is pick-ing us up and Lisa wants to know if you would like a ride home."

"But I thought I was going with Carmen."

"There was an unexpected development and Carmen had to leave early."

Ten minutes later, in a cold, light rain, Lee, Katie, and Lisa got into Lisa's mother's car and headed home. The girls felt sorry for Lee, though they had orchestrated the entire plan themselves. Quite simply, they had used him as a pawn to make the older boy jealous. It was their sole motive for descending upon his home and getting him to take Carmen to the dance. But oddly, after piecing together what had happened, Lee was more relieved than angry. For the past few weeks he had been forced to spend more time with these girls than he did with his actual friends, but alone now in the back seat of Lisa's mother's car, he felt safe again in his own skin.

The house looked deserted. The drapes were drawn, the driveway had a fresh dusting of snow, and the morning newspaper poked out bravely from the bushes. It had been two weeks since Jim's suspension from school, and with no further news, Lee was determined to find out what was up. He leaped onto the porch, took a deep breath, and knocked on the door.

"Are you here to collect, son?" Mr. Miller asked, blinking through his small round spectacles.

"Oh, no Sir. This is for you." He wedged the newspaper through the narrow slot of the open door.

"You're from school," Mr. Miller exclaimed with a sudden look of pride. "You were on Jim's basketball team." He opened the door wider to let Lee in. They moved through the house into the kitchen, where Mr. Miller motioned for Lee to sit at a small table.

"I don't suppose you've seen Jim for a while," he began in an oddly cheerful tone, "but if you know'd him like we do, you'd know he's not always easy to fig-ure. Don't know what he wants but he's always tryin' to find it." Mr. Miller walked over to the stove and turned on the burner.

"Cowboy coffee," Lee thought, hearing his mother's

voice chortling in his head. It was as if Mr. Miller had actually said, "I make a fresh pot every week whether I need to or not." Lee treasured the private jokes he shared with his mother.

"That boy ain't never satisfied, though we've tried hard to accommodate him."

Lee wondered about that. Jim never said much about his family, though he sometimes mentioned a brother, five years older. Rumor had it that he had been a delinquent and the Millers had disowned him.

"You kids nowadays got it easy, with no chores after school. I'd say it's all that time on your hands that leads to the trouble." He fished out a cigarette from a pack on the table. "I don't begrudge you your freedom, but keep your shirttails tucked in and your name out of the papers."

He took his first drag and poured himself some coffee. As he droned on, Lee surveyed the kitchen. Nearly every inch of wall, counter, and table space had been given over to knickknacks, portraits, and kitsch in a mishmash of clashing motifs and warring aesthetics. A map of the thirteen colonies and their adjacent territories had been framed in varnished wood and prominently displayed near the kitchen table; a studio photograph of Vivien Leigh had been taped to the side of a cupboard; and on the far wall was a large print depicting four dogs sitting at a table playing cards, drinks and smokes at hand. Most striking to Lee, however, was a pair of salt and pepper shakers shaped like human figures. The salt shaker took the form of a plump woman attired in a red and white checkered skirt, a white apron, and a red bandanna; the pepper container resembled a skinny, ragged farmhand. The woman carried a basket, the man held a rake. Both had skin as dark as charcoal.

These curious items and the old man's folksy speech made Lee feel that he had stepped into the past, yet this was the home in which the boldest and most forward-looking person Lee had ever known had been raised.

"Where is he?" Lee blurted out, fearing he was losing his nerve.

"He's in school," Mr. Miller replied. "We sent him upstate to a special place where he will get the attention he deserves."

"Special place." "Upstate." "Attention he deserves." Code words, Lee was sure, for some kind of reform school. "He's not coming back?" Lee asked weakly.

"Son, a boy gets caught messin' up bad and he's got to go away to get his head set on straight. Jim ain't comin' back to no school without discipline."

Lee had heard enough. He put his hands on the table and pushed himself to a standing position. "You'll see," Mr. Miller said. "He'll come out of this better than ever."

s the bus pulled into the parking lot of Jefferson Junior High, past the garbage receptacles, the boiler room, and the shipping and receiving doors, Lee felt the oddness of other people's lives. Compared to Wilford Creek, with its large windows, bright corridors, and spacious classrooms, Jefferson was dark and foreboding. It had been the district's first school, built over sixty years ago when a graduating class was barely twenty students. Class photos from yesteryear still hung in the hallways, giving Lee the creepy feeling of trespassing on ancient ruins.

It also didn't improve his frame of mind that Jefferson's basketball team was led by Thomas Warner, already a legend on the playground. His most enthusiastic supporters, chiefly his parents, his teachers, and, oddly, a short man with a large camera who took photos at every home game, all believed that Warner would be an all-American someday. To Lee, prone to let his imagination run wild, everything at Jefferson seemed like a backdrop to his greatness: the janitors made their rounds for him, the teachers taught their classes, and the cooks prepared and served the meals, all so that the day would proceed in an orderly fashion and Warner would be free to play basketball after school.

The locker room was hot. The team had to descend two rows of concrete steps to reach it. The ceilings were low and the air was stale. Coach took off his jacket, though sweat had already created blotchy patches on the back of his shirt. As the five starters sat on a narrow bench listening to Coach's instructions, their clammy legs kept brushing against those of their teammates.

Being on the court did not improve matters. Without Jim around, Lee was always less sure of himself. It helped, however, that Coach told him that his main role today would be to guard Warner, for it is easier to focus on defense when you are nervous. You merely lock onto your opponent and follow him wherever he goes.

At the end of the first quarter, Warner had not scored a basket, and the game was tied 12-12. At halftime, Jefferson led by three points and Warner had scored only a single free throw. Lee now thought they could win. Still, the second half was largely a repeat of the first. Jefferson was cold, but their free throws and pressing defense kept them in the lead. Lee held Warner to two baskets, but one of his teammates scored thirteen points and Jefferson held on to win. Still, Lee was pleased. Without Jim, they had played their best game of the year.

PART II

You go to school for weeks and everyday it's the same routine: classes, homework, tests, classes, homework, tests. Then just when you think you can't stand it anymore, the teachers ease up, decorate their rooms, and host parties. Before you know it, school is out. Christmas holidays, midyear break! And the freedom feels great.

For about a day.

By the second day, you're bored to death. In Northern cities, December is not a pretty month. If there's been snow, it's been shoveled into big piles alongside the roads, a sooty mix of snow and ice, garbage and road salt. When that mix melts, re-freezes, and thaws again, you walk through a dirty slop that leaves white rings on your shoes and boots. Cars wear a cummerbund of filth. Pants can be worn only once before they need washing. Pets stay inside. And unless you love cold weather, you stay inside too.

There were exceptions, of course. Little kids played in the snow, tough guys played hockey, and girls, well, girls continued to enjoy their privileged lives. At night, Lee would see them skating at the outdoor ice rink near City Hall, bundled up in their wool sweaters, colorful scarves, and oversized earmuffs, circling the rink gracefully to Christmas carols blaring from the municipal speakers. No doubt they would be looking forward to hot chocolate and marshmallows, sleepovers, and the hectic joy of helping their mothers bake cookies and complete the holiday shopping.

Christmas day at Lee's house was not much different than it was in other homes. First, it is hard to believe that the day has arrived, that another year has passed and that everyone, pretty much unchanged, is following familiar patterns and routines. Since Lee was an only child, there was not the near hysteria one often finds in homes with many children. His mother would be up the earliest, making coffee, and not much later there would be a little eggnog laced with something more bracing. Lee didn't pay much attention to that because he neither ate nor drank until he opened his presents. Since his family had started the day early, they then had the rest of the morning to take things easy. One Christmas morning Lee's father helped him put together a model airplane; on another, an intricate train set. Lee saw another side of his father on the holidays— someone capable of enjoying life.

The second half of the day was always a letdown, and sometimes a severe one. As relatives came to visit, or Lee's family went off to visit them, there was always an obligation to dress up; to bring presents and food; to be unnaturally cheerful; to be forced to interact with cousins one barely knew; to have to answer to aunts and uncles' prying questions; to pose for pictures; to eat food that had been laid out hours before; to use cups and silverware that didn't seem entirely clean; to sit in cramped, overheated living rooms near prickly trees pretending to be amused by toddlers who could neither walk nor talk, or if they did, did so badly; to see drooling babies chuck up their bottles and cry at the overstimulation; to smell men who had worked up a good day's odor; to feel, finally, that if one did not soon remove one's tight shoes and the pants that were pressing in at the waist and the white shirt that had already lost a button, that if one did not immediately have a place to stretch out and close one's eyes in private, then one just might have to get up and leave on one's own.

What kept the adults going was no mystery. Feeling no pain is more than just a cliche. When they would finally leave, a good two hours after it would have been more gracious and merciful to do so, there were again the obligatory hugs and promises to get together, which would not be met, and then it was out into the cold winter air once more, even less welcoming now with the sun long gone and a bitter chill in the air and the leather car seats cold and everyone tired and cranky from a lack of sleep and a surfeit of holiday cheer.

After Christmas and in the days leading up to New Year's, the earth freezes fast for winter. The upside is that without more snow, the sloppiness disappears. The world is as hard as a nut and people realize that if they take it as it is, it's not so bad. Even going out into this frozen tundra is not as difficult as it seemed a couple weeks earlier. There's a zest and a purity to the air that is invigorating.

On a cold Thursday morning, Lee and his friends headed over to the pool hall, relieved to be away from home. They hadn't so much as stretched their legs properly since vacation began. Lee brought his basketball, so after an hour of pool they stopped at the outdoor court at the high school. Fortunately, it was clear of snow, but there were several icy spots. After taking a few awkward shots, they removed their coats and gloves and began to move with more freedom and grace. It felt good to be using their muscles again. Tom had been playing basketball since sixth grade, and although he used to tower over his classmates, they were catching up to him. Brad was a flashy player who always looked better in pick-up games than he did in organized competition. He had a great shot and a flair for dribbling but wasn't much for passing or defense. Mike was a good athlete but was considered by many to be "muscle bound," which was either an explanation or rationalization for his lack of finesse.

Playing what the older boys called commando basketball, in which grabbing, holding, and pushing were all deemed fair play, it was far more physical than their typical games, and the icy conditions made even the simplest moves difficult. They thus took extremely long shots that sometimes, improbably, went in but also missed many of the easy ones, laughing so hard that they sometimes collapsed on the blacktop. They quit only after expending all of the energy that they had stored up during break, collecting their coats and gloves and heading for the donut shop where they argued about who won the most games, who missed the most shots, and who made the most awkward plays. For Lee, it was the first time he'd really enjoyed himself since Jim's suspension.

Returning to school after the holidays is depressing. After all, school is tolerable only in the fall, and even then for just a few short weeks. Fresh off summer break, students are eager to see classmates who had been on vacation all summer or who had been hunkered down in their own neighborhoods. They are also excited, and a little nervous, about advancing to a higher grade. But returning to school in winter is like coming back to a ghost town that had been abandoned in great haste. Damaged and worn furniture has been piled high in dark corridors; emergency exits are locked and chained; calendars are stuck on December; and bulletin boards stubbornly promote events that have long since passed. It usually takes several weeks to shake off the torpor of winter and the stale routines of the previous semester.

This winter, however, Lee was happy to be back at school, as his mother's long work hours and his father's frequent business trips left him alone for hours. There is a limit, he discovered, to how much television one can watch, and lacking better alternatives, he had been reduced to reading books from his mother's library, a tattered collection of commercially popular novels that didn't always make sense to him and at times seemed utterly bizarre: "The first time she kissed him," one passage read, "it was the taste of it that lingered in her mouth. The taste was like the taste of water, clear, cool, and a little bitter, and the feeling it left in her was as if she had been drinking a sweet, cold drink and then had to face the heat of a summer afternoon."

The girls arrived in twos and threes and stood just inside the gym door while the boys were still practicing. They were the finalists for the second semester cheerleading squad, which would be selected after today's tryout. Their presence in the gym created a stir among the boys, a change of mood and a quickening of movement. Some of the guys were exhilarated by it, others unsettled.

Giddy with stress on this important day, the girls hugged each other and offered words of encouragement, for they had already prepared for the various roles they might be called upon to play: grateful winner, gracious loser, selfless supporter, empathetic friend. In doing so, their reactions to the day's outcomes would be just as performative as their routines, a practice that would smooth their path through life.

In the meantime, the boys faced their own challenge. Since the girls had staked out their warm-up area outside the boys' locker room, each of the players had to weave his way through their knotted pairings to reach it. How they did so was a telling measure of their maturity and confidence. Some were flirtatious, all smiles and good humor. They enjoyed seeing the girls in their shorts just at much as the girls liked seeing them in their sleeveless jerseys. Others walked past the girls with the stiff cadence of soldiers. Finally, there was Lee, whose usually bouncy walk took on an extra degree of springiness. Although he was eager to see Carmen, he could not make himself look in her direction. It was his only protection against turning red and embarrassing himself.

The world was made for basketball. The new gymnasium at Shelby Junior High had the shiniest floor Lee had ever seen. The court was long, and the bleachers were twice as high as those at Wilford Creek. The lights were bright, the floor springy. Everything was perfect except for the scoreboard, which, while securely mounted on the cement-block wall closest to the entrance, had not yet been wired. So what should have been a glittering display of multi-colored lights was drab and lifeless, necessitating that school officials keep time on a stopwatch and the score on a chalkboard.

The game began in a whirl. For some reason—possibly the bright lights, the crowd, or the flashy uniforms of the Shelby players—Lee was disoriented. After Shelby won the tip-off, he couldn't find his man, who was unfortunately cherry-picking. He immediately caught a long, looping pass from Shelby's best guard and scored the game's first two points.

"Get into the game," Lee said to himself. But things only got worse. Brad brought the ball down the court and took a rushed and awkward shot. Shelby got the rebound and headed the other way. Have you ever had the feeling that you weren't actually there? That's how Lee felt. All the important action seemed to be happening far away from him.

He finally touched the ball after Shelby scored their second basket. He in-bounded it to Brad, but this time Shelby surprised them with a press. Brad quickly passed the ball back to Lee, who wasn't ready for it. It bounced off his knee and went out of bounds. Coach called a time-out. Wilford Creek was behind 4-0, had just lost the ball, and was completely out of sync.

A time-out! Was there ever such a thing? You had merely 120 seconds to run to the bench, wipe off the sweat, take a swig of water, and listen to Coach's savage critique of everything you are doing wrong. But this time Coach was calm and measured. He was even amused by the situation. About the muffed pass, he merely said, "A guy could get hurt like that Lee." A joke from Coach was a rare treat, and everyone laughed. It also relaxed them. They played a lot better after that and actually won the game handily.

ee knew what was coming, as a flurry of academic deadlines always seemed to coincide with the end of basketball season. One of these assignments was for his English class, which at least seemed straight-forward enough: "From any magazine or anthology recognized for its good fiction, select a story you find interesting and would like to analyze." Mr. Rand, Lee's English teacher, had written the names of a few magazines, journals, and short story anthologies on the blackboard to help the students get started, but he was quick to point out that many of the stories they come across might be pitched above their reading level and life experience, so it would be a good idea to get their parents' advice to ensure that they made suitable selections. After finding a story they liked, they would then write a note to him outlining the story and discussing their interest in it. Lee appreciated this approach, as it allowed him to dip his toes into the water before committing to a full immersion.

Generally, Lee liked the way Mr. Rand taught his classes, which were more like conversations than lectures. Also, he placed more emphasis on the content of their writing than he did on their punctuation and grammar, though he emphasized that learning formal grammar was not optional. They could never be effective writers without it. There is a big difference, he pointed out, between the sentences, "Let's eat, grandma," and "Let's eat grandma!"

"Commas save lives" became the class's inside joke and a puzzling phrase to outsiders.

No matter the assignment, getting started is always the most difficult part. Sharpening pencils and adjusting your chair or headrest do not count. So on a Saturday morning, late in February, Lee headed over to the public library to see what he could find. He was immensely grateful that Mr. Rand had provided them with a list of magazines and books to start with. Otherwise he might have wasted a lot of time flipping through the pages of *Life, Time, Newsweek,* or even *Good Housekeeping* looking for good fiction. He got lucky almost immediately when he found a pile of *New Yorker* magazines in the basement stacks, a publication on Mr. Rand's list. They went back at least five years. Then, as if he were reaching for the winning ticket in a jar full of worthless ones, he pulled out an issue from the bottom of the pile, found a comfortable chair in the reading room, and got busy. He quickly found a story that looked interesting. After reading it twice, he wrote to his teacher:

First Note:

Mr. Rand, I am not sure you will approve of this story, or that I will be able to analyze it correctly. While I did find it in one of the magazines you recommended, I don't know if its author, John Updike, is considered a "serious" writer. I read his story "A&P" because I was curious how anyone could write a story about a grocery store. Even though it was weird, I ended up sort of liking it, but I am not sure if it is appropriate for this class. First, it sounds as if it were written by a teenager. And second, I am not sure you would consider it appropriate for our age group. It's about three girls walking into a grocery store in their bathing suits and the guys on the cash registers checking them out. Then one of the clerks, Sammy, gets fired or rather quits after his manager embarrasses the girls over the way they're dressed. There is a lot of description about how the girls look in their bathing suits, which is a little embarrassing to write about. Can you tell me whether this story is okay before I spend any more time on it?

Thank you,
Lee Rollins

Second Note:

Thank you for letting me decide whether I should discuss this story with my parents. I don't think I will. I understand a little better how some things in a story might be "deliberately provocative," as you put it, so I will try to keep that in mind. I never thought than an author would want to write something that sounded so immature. When I mentioned this to a friend, he replied that I obviously had never read *The Catcher in the Rye*.

You also asked us to look at the first sentence and try to determine "whether it seems effective in introducing various elements in the story, like the theme, content, point of view, and even the tone of the entire work." That's a lot to ask of one sentence! But this first sentence does do some of that. At first I thought it was ungrammatical or that there must be some missing words, but I finally realized that it does make sense. It goes, "In walks these three girls in nothing but bathing suits." Even though this grocery store is five miles from the ocean, the girls are not even wearing shoes. And the one who leads them around has let the straps of her bathing suit fall loosely off her shoulders (whether accidentally or not) allowing the top of her suit to slip a bit. Would that be provocative on her part? Or the author's? Maybe he has seen that kind of thing in real life, so he thought that he would put it in a story.

This is where I am stuck. Although these descriptions may be interesting to some readers, they aren't really anything new. Who hasn't seen a girl in a skimpy bathing suit? So what is the point? Maybe I could focus on how the boys react to the girls compared to how the manager reacts and then try to figure out why Sammy quits over such a stupid thing. You said we should also examine the style of the writing. This story is very fast-paced and jumpy, which is occasionally hard to follow. Would that be considered a "style"? And there is alliteration in the first sentence, something we talked about in our unit on poetry. I thought that was just a poetry thing. Anyway, my main goal will be trying to figure out why there is such a big deal made over something so unimportant.

Thanks,
Lee Rollins

PART III

Finally, after what seemed like an eternity of snow, bitter winds, icy sidewalks, and oppressive darkness, winter faded into memory and spring arrived for real. In the interval between the end of school day and the start of baseball and track practice, a cluster of students mingled on the worn path between the school and the baseball diamond. Yet despite their camaraderie, they were eager to head for home. Freedom was in the air, and the approaching summer promised more liberty yet.

Delayed by a jammed locker, Lee finally exited the school by the boys' locker room, stepping out into the brilliant sunshine. Shielding his eyes, he made his way down the short walkway until nearly tripping over the long legs of Carmen, who with Lisa, was leaning against a bicycle rack.

"Lee, how are you?" Lisa exclaimed. "We've been looking all over for you!" He didn't answer, having learned that nervous people can keep a conversation going all on their own. Proving him right, she continued: "I swear, we're going to show up at your house again!"

But Carmen protested: "Don't worry, Lee. We won't bother you anymore."

His heart melted. It is easy to hold a grudge when someone hurts you, but harder to stay angry when they are truly sorry. It also seemed pointless. How could anyone be unhappy on a day like this?

They were on the freeway going sixty. Lee sat in the backseat with Carmen. Her mother was alone in the front. It felt like summer already. The top was down on the red Ford convertible and the wind was whipping through Lee and Carmen's hair. Carmen had talked her mother into taking them to the state university where her sister was a sophomore. What she didn't tell her mother was that they were also planning on seeing Jim, whose new school was nearby, and with any luck, they just might be bringing him home.

As they drove through the town of South Hadley, taking in its quaint and brightly painted shops, cafes, and specialty stores, Lee couldn't help comparing it to the sprawling array of bowling alleys, car washes, and beauty parlors in his own town, where you could find a bar or party store on nearly every corner but couldn't find a bookstore or decent restaurant if your life depended on it.

Just beyond South Hadley they entered the university district, a utopia of lush and spacious lawns, turreted buildings, and stone walkways. Students threw Frisbees, played football, and lay in the sun. Even those who were reading or feverishly writing in thick, spiral notebooks seemed in harmony with the day. If this is college, Lee thought, you could sign him up now. Yet not five minutes later, in the parking lot behind her mammoth dormitory, Carmen's sister cast a large shadow over Lee's sunny disposition. Still dressed for winter in a turtleneck, sweater, and boots, and looking as pale and dispirited as a slug, she was annoyed that they had arrived early. Saturday was her laundry day—didn't they know!—and while she washed and dried her clothes, she got her studying done.

"Where are your books?" she asked Carmen, as if her sister had made this three-hour drive to sit in a library.

"Lizzie, honey," Carmen's mother interjected, "Lee and Carmen are here to see the university. This is Lee's first visit, you know?"

"Well, what does he want to see?" she asked, without even glancing in his direction.

"Elisabeth, put yourself in their place. They want to be outside. They want to walk around and enjoy themselves."

"But you said Carmen needed help with her math."

"She does, but that can wait. Let them explore the campus first and you and I can go shopping."

Appeased for the moment, Elizabeth paraded them through her dormitory, stopping to show off the TV room, the study areas, the basement laundry, and the snack machines. She then led them up the north stairwell to her third-floor double, surprising her roommate,

Donna, who had just returned from the shower. An awkward conversation ensued, as predictable as the dorm's hard mattresses and the cafeteria's bland cuisine. In short order, the visitors were shooed away so Donna could change, after which they all went to the Student Union to eat. By twelve-thirty lunch was over, the shuttle tickets had been secured, and the ambitious schemers were on their own.

Carmen took the lead. They wouldn't even need the shuttle. They merely had to walk to the southeast boundary of the university and merge onto Main Street. Here they would walk the four blocks of shops, pubs, and restaurants until they hit Cass Avenue, which would take them to the outskirts of town and the entrance to the Covington Military Academy. At home it had been easy to imagine that all Jim needed was a little moral support and the three of them could slip away unnoticed. Carmen had concocted the plan herself, but reality proved bumpier than her fantasy. A ten-foot iron gate blocked the entrance, and a barbed wire fence enclosed the property. Clearly, the carefree and fun-loving vibe of the college town stopped there.

Carmen pressed the buzzer, the gate opened, and the intrepid pair trudged up a narrow driveway. When they reached the top, a young man in dress uniform stepped out of a small booth to greet them. He issued them passes and suggested that they might find Jim behind an adjacent building where the cadets without visitors went for privacy.

He was right. Free from the eyes of their superiors, six cadets, sans blazers, were playing football. Sporting a crew cut that left no trace of his once curly hair, Jim looked like his older brother whose photograph Lee had seen atop the Millers' TV. But that was the least surprising thing about him. After he had been sent away—actually, until this very moment—Lee had envisioned him sinking into a world of gray days and even bleaker nights, with the thought of escape his only comfort. Yet here he was, their exiled friend, having the time of his life.

"Never figured you two for the military," he teased once he had gotten over the shock of seeing them. It would have been difficult to say who was happier, he or they, but the mere sight of him was everything that Lee and Carmen had hoped it would be. Still, after the emotional waves receded, their spirited conversation quickly lost its easy flow. They described their short time at the university and answered his questions about home. However, they were mum about their plan to rescue him, so silly it now seemed.

Sensing their uneasiness, he showed them around. Having no previous knowledge of military schools or the military in general, Lee was impressed with the neatness and order of the place and its strong sense of purpose, but its tightly defined hierarchy, spartan accommodations, uniformity of dress, and restrictions on individual expression were so alien and objectionable to him he wondered how they could be amenable to his friend. Wasn't this the same person who had instigated a midnight raid on the girls' cabin during sixth-grade camp, the young hooligan who had smuggled in a six-pack into a seventh-grade sleepover, and more recently, the rebel who spoke of running away, hitchhiking to California and living on the beach? No, apparently he wasn't. While they were home playing Hardy Boys and Nancy Drew, he was here shooting actual rifles.

"Well, when do you get out?" Lee finally asked, assuming that Jim would be coming home for the summer.

"I'm not sure," he responded.

In truth, he was ambivalent himself. After his father had delivered him to the Commanding Officer this past December and practically signed his life away, he felt like he was in prison. All he could think about was returning home. But his life had changed so much in the past few months, he was at a loss to put it into words.

"What do you mean?" Carmen shouted. "They can't keep you all summer."

"No, they can't," he quickly agreed, "but every July they offer a course in survival training, and if I take it and survive (here he smiled, looking like the Jim they knew so well) I could earn points for next year."

There was no disguising their disappointment now.

"Guys, it's hard to explain. I hated it here for the first few weeks. Boot camp was worse than you could imagine, but the other cadets have accepted me now and my superior officer thinks I might make a good soldier."

Lee finally understood. Jim needed purpose and direction, and the military was all too happy to provide it. He was the kind of person who would enjoy parachuting out of an airplane into enemy territory, running under fire to the next barricade, or throwing a grenade through an open window. Although they had been inseparable friends and teammates the past few years, there was a fundamental difference in their temperaments that was turning them into vastly different people.

The ride home was dreamlike. The sun was setting, the first soft sunset of the season, turning the horizon into various shades of pink. Above these cotton-candy wisps, a few cumulus clouds remained, snow white to steel gray, making the sky look solid and substantial. When he had left home that morning, Lee was fired with purpose. He knew what his life was about—rescuing Jim and restoring their shattered lives—but in a flash he realized his mistake. Jim was not in prison. He was in heaven. Instead of confining him, the military was giving him everything he needed, and so with Jim a lost cause, Carmen would probably be moving on as well. Lee's dream had been a fantasy, as most dreams usually are. He knew he couldn't keep courting disappointment, longing for things that could never be, so he closed his eyes and leaned his head against the seat in front of him. Feeling the car's vibrations, he imagined himself traveling at supersonic speed. He was surging ahead, rocketing towards his future. He might as well enjoy the ride.

By Thursday the ninth of June, the temperature at noon had already passed eighty degrees. It was the final day of school and Lee's social studies teacher, Mrs. Ray, was collecting textbooks and passing back old papers. Just that morning a light breeze from an open window had lulled Lee into a heavy-lidded slumber, but now as Mrs. Ray directed her students in a flurry of housekeeping duties, he was as alert as a sentry. The classroom's unused supplies—paper clips, glue, tacks, pencils, and construction paper—had been gathered and transported to a storage closet down the hall, all the desktops had been washed, and a year's worth of petrified chewing gum had been scraped from the underside of the study carrels.

Finally, with just a half hour to go before the final bell, on Lee's last day of junior high school, Mrs. Ray led her charges into the hall to remove the remaining debris from their lockers. Strangely, however, having been rambunctious all morning, they were now subdued, as if a sedative had been injected into their milk cartons. It was finally sinking in that a new redistricting plan would be splitting their class in half. Some would be attending the old high school while others would be sent to the new one.

Teary-eyed, the girls kept stopping one another for hugs.

Lee wanted no part of it. If he had learned anything in school, it was to keep his feelings to himself. Just three years before, his sixth-grade teacher, the aptly named Mr. Wise, asked if anyone in his class would be willing to transfer to the other sixth-grade section. That class, led by the spunky Miss Maryanne Kerr, had already lost one student to illness and another to relocation, with a third slated to move away in the spring. Responding to Mr. Wise's request, Lee jokingly raised his hand. Everyone knew, he thought, how happy he was to be in this class. His best friends were here, and he had bonded with a teacher who was also his first basketball coach.

But on Monday morning, Mr. Wise announced that Lee would be transferring to the other section. Lee could no longer remember much of what happened next except for standing at Mr. Wise's desk, in full view of his classmates, fighting back tears and trying to explain that he had only been kidding. Although he was eventually allowed to stay in Mr. Wise's class, the damage had been done. Apparently, his favorite teacher had no misgivings about sending him to the other section. Walking home with a friend that day, Lee tried to explain his reaction, but he was unable to express what he did not fully understand: the extent to which the classroom had become his family.

So there would be no emotional leave-taking now,

though Carmen had been hovering in his vicinity all morning. During science class, she had joined him at the sink to wash out the test tubes and beakers. At lunch, she and Katie had sat at his table, and now, once again, she was heading his way.

"Hi," she said, beaming that beautiful smile.

"Hi," he repeated, cautiously. Despite everything, he was still leery of that smile. Like a postcard of a beautiful summer day, it seemed to promise more than it would ever deliver.

"I can't believe it," she told him excitedly, "Mrs. Ray had us hauling all of her books to her car. Lisa thinks she's retiring!" Lee didn't care. He knew that the teacher-student relationship only went so far. Then, sweeping his hand across the top shelf of his locker, he felt something he'd forgotten was there—an athletic sock knotted at the top and bulging with marbles.

"Hey, take this," he said, tossing it her way, but the heavy sock bag slipped from her fingers and hit the floor.

CRACK.

"Marbles!" Lee exclaimed, and they both laughed. They were the remnant of the hundreds that Jim had smuggled into school this past fall. He had spent all morning rolling them down the halls, wedging them into door jambs and window tracks, dropping them into toilets and sinks, and sending a couple dozen cascading across the cafeteria floor. After lunch, he forced a few through the narrow vents of the heat register in his math classroom, creating a clatter so loud that the teacher could not be heard. By the time the school's engineer arrived to loosen the screws, remove the fan's heavy lid, and with a needle-nose pliers painstakingly pluck them out one by one, Jim had given the remaining stash to Lee, who hid them in his locker. Jim's contraband thus vanished as quickly as it had appeared, and though he was closely observed for the rest of the day, he was never fingered for his crimes.

Carmen scooped out a handful. Cool to the touch, they glowed like precious treasure, but there was no time to savor it. The final bell had rung and the teachers were dismissing their classes. What would have pleased Jim the most, like their dumping the remaining sockful into the school's boiler or pounding a few into the treads of some stupid teacher's car, was now impossible. Instead, Lee grabbed Carmen's hand and led her down the stairs. Pushing open the doors, they ran down the steps and stopped along the sidewalk. Lee dumped the marbles onto the lawn. There must have been a hundred, in living Technicolor: blues, whites, greens, reds, pinks, blacks, and silvers, all in dazzling combinations and patterns.

The school doors burst open and the students came rushing down the steps.

"Give them away!" Lee shouted to Carmen.

They stood on the lawn, arms extended. Leery

of tricks, the younger students veered away, but the ninth-graders, remembering Jim's prank, were delighted to have a souvenir. Held to the light, they glinted like tiny stars. Cradled in their palms, they wobbled like uncertain planets. These precious spheres, now slipped into pockets or dropped into book bags, would one day glow again, alive with the exuberance of adolescent eyes.